Walt Disney's Mother Goose

Story adapted by Monique Peterson
Pictures by The Walt Disney Studios
Adapted by Al Dempster

A WELCOME BOOK

Disney
EDITIONS

New York

HEY, DIDDLE, DIDDLE

Hey, diddle, diddle, the cat and the fiddle,
The cow jumped over the moon;
The little dog laughed to see such sport,
And the dish ran away with the spoon.

CROSS PATCH

Cross patch,
    draw the latch,
Sit by the fire
    and spin;
Take a cup and
    drink it up,
Then call your
    neighbors in.

JACK SPRAT

Jack Sprat would eat no fat,
His wife would eat no lean,
And so between the two of them,
They ate the platter clean.

LITTLE JACK HORNER

Little Jack Horner sat
  in a corner,
Eating his
  Christmas pie;
He stuck in his thumb
  and pulled out a plum,
And said, "What a good
  boy am I!"

LITTLE MISS MUFFET

Little Miss Muffet
Sat on a tuffet,
Eating her curds and whey.
There came a big spider,
Who sat down beside her,
And frightened Miss Muffet away!

HICKORY, DICKORY, DOCK

Hickory, dickory,
dock,
The mouse ran up the
clock.
The clock struck one,
The mouse ran down;
Hickory, dickory, dock!

LITTLE TOMMY TUCKER

Little Tommy Tucker
Sings before supper.
What shall he eat?
White bread and butter.

How shall he cut it
Without e'er a knife?
How shall he marry
Without e'er a wife?

GEORGIE PORGIE

Georgie Porgie,
  pudding and pie,
Kissed the girls and
  made them cry.
When the boys came
  out to play,
Georgie Porgie ran
  away.

LITTLE BETTY BLUE

Little Betty Blue
Lost her holiday shoe.
What shall poor
    Betty do?
Find her another
To match the other,
And then she'll walk
    in two.

JUMPING JOAN

Here am I, little
    Jumping Joan.
When nobody's with me,
I'm always alone.

DIDDLE, DIDDLE DUMPLING

Diddle, diddle dumpling, my son John,
Went to bed with his socks still on;
One shoe off and one shoe on,
Diddle, diddle dumpling, my son John.

FIVE TOES

This little piggy went
to market,
This little piggy
stayed home;
This little piggy
ate roast beef,
This little piggy had none;
This little piggy cried,
"Wee-wee-wee!"
All the way home.

MARY'S LAMB

Mary had a little lamb,
Its fleece was white as snow;
And everywhere that Mary went,
The lamb was sure to go.

It followed her to school one day,
Which was against the rule;
It made the children
laugh and play
To see a lamb at school.

ONE TO TEN

1, 2, 3, 4, 5,
I caught a
     hare alive;
6, 7, 8, 9, 10,
I let him go
     again.

THE QUEEN OF HEARTS

The Queen of Hearts,
She made some tarts,
All on a summer's day.
The Knave of Hearts,
He took those tarts,
And carried them away.

The King of Hearts,
Called for those tarts,
With a loud and royal roar.
The Knave of Hearts
Returned those tarts,
And vowed he'd take no more.

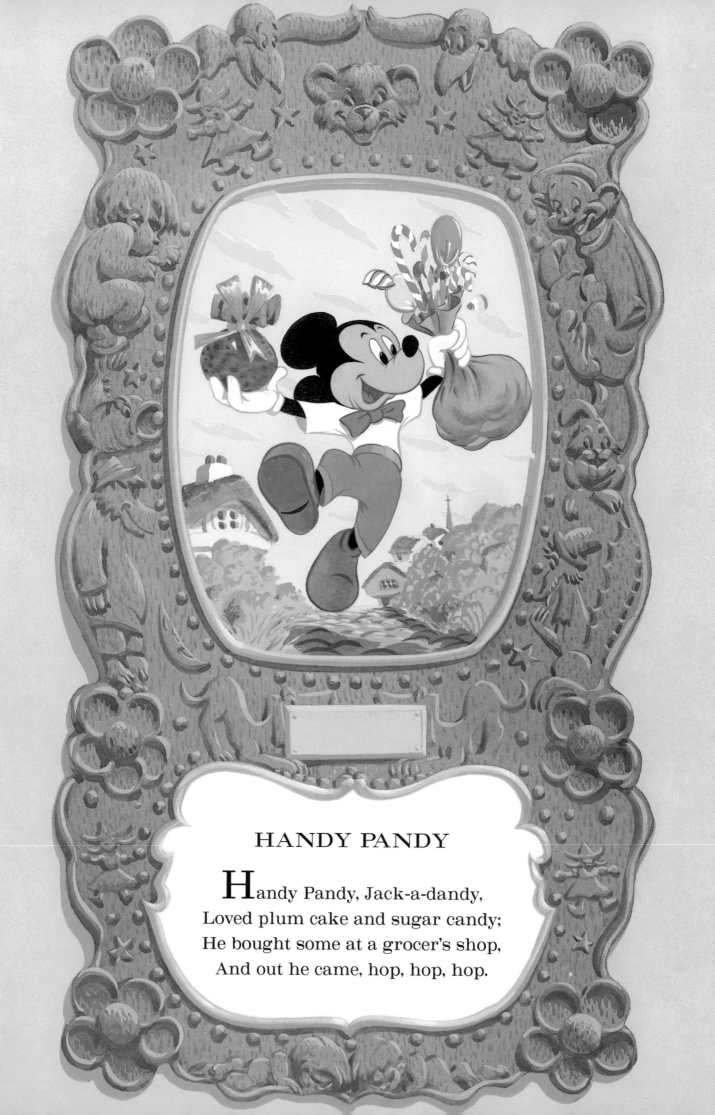

HANDY PANDY

Handy Pandy, Jack-a-dandy,
Loved plum cake and sugar candy;
He bought some at a grocer's shop,
And out he came, hop, hop, hop.

THIS IS THE WAY

This is the way the ladies ride,
Tri, tre, tre, tree, Tri, tre, tre, tree!
This is the way the ladies ride,
Tri, tre, tre, tre, tri-tre-tre-tree!

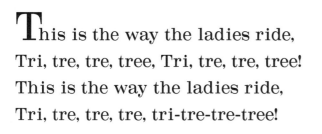

This is the way the cowboys ride,
Gallop-a-trot, gallop-a-trot!

This is the way the cowboys ride,
Gallop-a-gallop-a-trot!

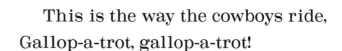

This is the way the farmers ride,
Hobbledy-hoy, hobbledy-hoy!
This is the way the farmers ride,
Hobbledy-hobbledy-hoy!

DING, DONG, BELL

Ding, dong, bell,
Kitty's in the well!
Who put her in?
Mean Tommy Linn.
Who pulled her out?
Little Johnny Stout.

What a prankish boy was that,
To try to scare poor kitty-cat,
Who never once did any harm,
But killed the mice in
    Father's barn!

A DILLAR,
A DOLLAR

A dillar, a dollar,
A ten o'clock scholar,
What makes you
   come so soon?
You used to come
   at ten o'clock,
And now you come
   at noon.

BOBBY SHAFTOE

Bobby Shaftoe's gone to sea,
Silver buckles at his knee;
He'll come back and marry me,
Handsome Bobby Shaftoe!

THERE WERE TWO BLACKBIRDS

There were two
blackbirds,
Sitting on a hill,
The one named Jack,
The other named Bill.

Fly away, Jack!
Fly away, Bill!
Come again, Jack!
Come again, Bill!

OLD KING COLE

Old King Cole was a merry old soul,
And a merry old soul was he;
He called for his pipe, he called for his bowl,
And he called for his musicians three!

IF I'D AS MUCH MONEY

If I'd as much money as I could spend,
I never would cry, "Old chairs to mend!
Old chairs to mend! Old chairs to mend!"
I never would cry, "Old chairs to mend!"

HUSH-A-BYE

Hush-a-bye, baby,
On the treetop;
When the wind blows,
The cradle will rock;
When the bough breaks,
The cradle will fall;
And down will come baby,
Cradle and all.

RUB A DUB DUB

Rub a dub dub,
Three men in a tub,
And who could they
    possibly be?
The butcher, the baker,
The candlestick maker,
Sailing the salty sea.

THERE WAS AN OLD WOMAN

There was an old woman who flew up in a basket,
Seventeen times as high as the moon;
And where she was going, I couldn't but ask her,
But I saw that she carried a broom.

"Old woman, old woman, old woman," said I,
"O whither, O whither, O whither so high?"
"To sweep the cobwebs off the sky!"
"Shall I go with you?" "Yes, by and by."

BONNY LASS, BONNY LASS

Bonny lass, bonny lass,
Wilt thou be mine?
Thou shalt not wash dishes
Nor yet feed the swine,
But sit on a cushion
And sew a fine seam,
And feed upon strawberries,
Sugar and cream.

THE OLD WOMAN
WHO LIVED IN A SHOE

There was an old woman who lived in a shoe;

She had so many children she didn't know what to do.

She gave them some broth and two slices of bread;

She kissed them all fondly, then sent them to bed.

HUMPTY DUMPTY

Humpty Dumpty sat on a wall,
Humpty Dumpty had a great fall;
All the king's horses and all the king's men
Couldn't put Humpty Dumpty together again.

THREE WISE MEN OF GOTHAM

Three wise men of Gotham
Went to sea in a bowl;
If the bowl had been stronger,
My song would be longer.

JACK BE NIMBLE

Jack be nimble,
Jack be quick,
Jack jump over
the candlestick.

PUSSYCAT, PUSSYCAT

"Pussycat, pussycat, where
have you been?"
"I've been to London to look at
the Queen."
"Pussycat, pussycat, what
did you there?"
"I frightened a little mouse
under the chair."

SIMPLE SIMON

Simple Simon met a pieman,
Going to the fair;
Says Simple Simon to the pieman,
"Let me taste your ware."

Says the pieman to Simple Simon,
"Show me first your penny."
Says Simple Simon to the pieman,
"Indeed I haven't any."

He went to catch a dickeybird,
And thought he could not fail,
Because he'd got a little salt
To put upon his tail.

Simple Simon went a-fishing,
And tried to catch a whale;
But all the water he could find
Was in his mother's pail.

He scooped up water in a sieve,
But soon it all ran through;
And now poor Simple Simon
Bids you all adieu!

WEE WILLIE WINKIE

Wee Willie Winkie runs
through the town,
Upstairs and downstairs,
in his nightgown;
Rapping at each window,
crying down the block,
"Are all the children in their beds,
for now it's eight o'clock!"

BYE, BABY BUNTING

Bye, baby bunting,
Father's gone a-hunting,
Mother's gone a-milking,
Sister's gone a-silking,
And brother's gone to buy a skin
To wrap the baby bunting in.

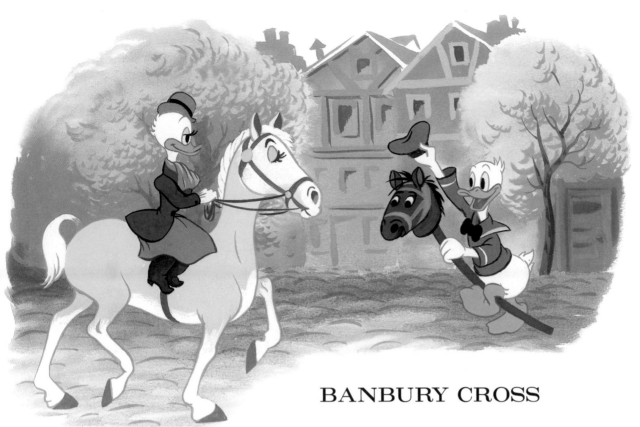

BANBURY CROSS

Ride a cockhorse to Banbury Cross,
To see a fine lady upon a white horse.
Rings on her fingers and bells on her toes,
She shall have music wherever she goes.

HOT CROSS BUNS

Hot cross buns!
Hot cross buns!
One a penny, two a penny,
Hot cross buns!

If you have no daughters,
Give them to your sons.
One a penny, two a penny,
Hot cross buns!

LITTLE BOY BLUE

Little boy blue, come blow your horn,
The sheep's in the meadow, the cow's in the corn.
Where is the boy who looks after the sheep?
He's under a haycock fast asleep.
Will you wake him?
No, not I,
For if I do,
He's sure to cry.

BLOW, WIND, BLOW

Blow, wind, blow!
    And go, mill, go!
That the miller may
    grind his corn;
That the baker
    may take it,
And into bread
    make it,
And bring us a loaf
    in the morn.

PAT-A-CAKE

Pat-a-cake, pat-a-cake,
Baker's man,
Bake me a cake
As fast as you can.
Roll it, and prick it,
And mark it with a B,
Then put it in the oven
For Baby and me.

PETER, PETER, PUMPKIN EATER

Peter, Peter,
pumpkin eater,
Had a wife and
couldn't feed her;
He put her in a
pumpkin shell,
And there he kept her
very well.

SING A SONG
OF SIXPENCE

Sing a song of sixpence,
A pocket full of rye;
Four-and-twenty blackbirds
Baked into a pie!

When the pie was opened
The Birds began to sing;
Wasn't that a dainty dish
To set before the King?